Devil's Fork

AN AGGIE ADVENTURE

D.L. WINCHESTER

Undertaker Books

UNDERTAKER BOOKS
www.undertakerbooks.com

Praise for Devil's Fork

*"A solidly told, diverse Western tale, rife with dark humor and demons; Devil's Fork is an irresistible read. In a sequel even better than the first, with more Aggie and more adventure, Winchester makes the Western horror trope feel fresh."*Desiree Horton, author of *Midnight Mother*

"Raw, uncompromising, and sharp as a razorblade, Aggie is back and ready to go to war."
C.M. Saunders, author of *Silent Mine* and *Blood Lake*

"Devil's Fork calls out to Blatty as much as it does to Cormac McCarthy. A desolate ride through the New Mexico desert where demons leer from the shadows and the stakes are higher than just a handful of gold. Winchester spins one hell of a yarn."
- Brennan LaFaro, author of *Noose*

"In the gritty and largely lawless West, a young woman tougher than everyone around her must battle demonic forces that threaten to overwhelm and consume every human soul on Earth. In Devil's Fork, D.L. Winchester delivers a horror story as grand in scale as the western sky, and as unsparing as the landscape itself."
Ann O'Mara Heyward, Award-winning short story author

For Anna

Devil's Fork
An Aggie Adventure

Chapter 1

The dark clouds had blown in quickly, catching Aggie by surprise.

She was riding through northern New Mexico, putting as much distance as she could between her and the remote Utah canyon where her papa, Roche, lay buried.

In a way, the clouds reflected her mood: dark, stormy, full of anger.

She hadn't had enough time with him.

It was supposed to be their last job, a quick trip to Briar Hill to get the Spencer brothers, collect the reward, and then they'd head for Aggie's hometown of Ojinaga, Mexico, for Roche's reunion with her mother.

A reunion that couldn't happen now.

Instead, Aggie was riding alone for Ojinaga, on the banks of the Rio Grande at the bottom of the river's big bend, to tell her mother Roche was dead.

The trail led into a canyon, steep cliffs carved by the river next to her. Aggie's horse plodded into it, knowing the rain was coming and any form of shelter would be through the canyon. Aggie watched the water, flowing fast over and around the rocks.

A flash flood would ruin her day.

The rain started falling as she rounded a bend to see a plain stretching before her. To her right, the river plunged over a waterfall. Up a small trail to her left, a large opening in the canyon wall that had to be a cave entrance.

She turned her horse, a grullo quarter horse she'd named Gato, up the trail as the rain increased in intensity. Riding into the cave, she swung off her horse and looked around her new shelter.

It was about thirty feet deep, with a high ceiling. The floor was smooth, the rock worn down by the river before it rerouted over the falls.

It was primitive, but it was adequate to wait out the storm.

Aggie reached into her saddlebag and took out a handful of beef jerky. If she was going to be stuck here, she might as well eat. Sitting on the floor, she leaned against the cave wall and stared out into the rain as she chewed.

She missed Roche.

The rain felt like a reflection of her heart the previous few weeks, trying to pretend like her life hadn't been changed all over again. It had taken sixteen years for her to work up the nerve to leave her little village on the Rio Grande to go looking for her father, and two years to find him. After that, she'd spent six months nursing him back to health after a pair of bandits left him for dead in a Wyoming valley, then another two years riding with him as his bounty hunting partner.

Getting to know the man her mother had fallen in love with had been an amazing experience, one that made her want to get him back home to her mom more than anything.

But now he was dead, she was riding alone, and the dark clouds that had matched her anger had turned loose in a way Aggie would never allow herself to do.

After she ate, Aggie realized the storm wasn't going to pass quickly. Getting to her feet, she took her saddle off her horse, then put her bedroll against the wall and leaned back.

Gato lay down for a rest as Aggie walked to the entrance. It had been late afternoon when the storm came up, and she'd been hoping to reach the town of Devil's Fork before dark. If the storm didn't pass, she'd have to bed down here.

Well, not *have to*, but riding in the rain wasn't fun, and Gato wouldn't appreciate it either.

Thunder rolled across the sky, and a new noise joined the sound of the storm.

Hoofbeats.

Aggie tensed. For a woman traveling alone, company wasn't always a good thing. She was adept with her pistol, but if the rider wasn't alone, she might end up in a difficult situation. Even though she didn't look like a woman in her button-down shirt and pants, her gender would be obvious as soon as she opened her mouth.

She'd had to put her boot up the asses of several men who'd tried to take liberties with her, and cleaning the shit off was never a good time.

A shape appeared in the wall of water, and a moment later, a man, water dripping off his hat, led his soaked horse into the cave.

"Oh! Hello! I didn't realize someone else had taken shelter here. The Good Lord seems to think I need a bath," he said, taking off his hat and shaking the water from it. "Do you mind if I join you?"

His question caught her off guard. Most men would assume the right to share the cave until the storm had passed.

Then she saw the faded black cassock he wore. "Of course, Padre." She reached for his hand and kissed it.

He smiled. "Hello, child."

"It's Aggie, Padre," she said.

The priest nodded. "Of course, Aggie. I've been serving missions near Junction City, in the northwestern part of New Mexico, but I'm on my way back to Santa Fe."

Aggie nodded, studying him. He was about her height, lean, with white hair and the tan skin of a Hispanic. His brown eyes were kind, and she instinctively trusted him.

"I was hoping to get to Devil's Fork tonight, but I don't think this rain is going to let up."

"Perhaps it's for the best," Padre said. "There are rumors that evil lurks in Devil's Fork. The bishop has made it clear his priests are not to pass a night in the town. But this cave should be far enough away to satisfy him, don't you think?"

Aggie nodded. Damn, this priest liked to talk. Not that she minded. It had been over a week since she'd heard a voice other than her own.

"Do you usually travel in men's clothes?" he asked, undoing his saddle and setting it on the floor of the cave.

"It's a useful defense mechanism," she said, a smile creeping onto her face.

"I suppose it's practical, though I imagine that pistol you're carrying is more convincing," he said. "Although as pretty as you are, I'm surprised a man isn't traveling with you."

She paused, thinking of her papa. "One was."

Padre saw the look on her face, and must have recognized it as grief. "I'm sorry. I know losing a loved one is painful."

She nodded, remembering her father's body spread out on the torture table at the Screaming House. "The men who killed him... They tortured my papa before they..." Tears rolled down her cheeks.

His hand reached for her shoulder. "It's alright, my child."

Aggie nodded. "Thank you." She let out a deep breath. "I didn't catch your name."

"And yet you've been using it this whole time," he said, allowing a touch of humor to enter his voice. "I am a priest, so I go by Padre."

A smile. "You don't have a real name?"

He winked. "My mother, may her memory be blessed, made a choice I am not fond of. So I prefer to be addressed by my title."

Aggie laughed in spite of herself. "Okay, Padre."

He returned the smile. "I trust your father's killers were brought to justice?"

She thought about her time outside the Screaming House, remembering the reports from her gun as she sent the defenders of that vile place to the fires of hell. "I arranged for them to discuss their sins with a friend of yours."

A flicker of amusement appeared in Padre's eyes. "I see." He said something in Latin, then crossed himself. "I pray for your father's soul, and your own."

"Thank you," Aggie said.

Padre waved a hand. "It's my job. I also bless horses, and yours is a fine specimen."

Aggie smiled, grateful for the subject change. "I call him Gato."

"Cat?" the priest asked.

"He doesn't like them very much. He tries to grab their tails with his teeth."

A grin crossed Padre's face. "We will get along well then, your horse and I."

Trinidad, Colorado, six months earlier

"What are you going to do when I'm gone?" Roche asked her.

They were watching a ranch where a group of bank robbers was hiding out.

"What do you mean?" Aggie asked, looking confused.

Roche smiled. "I'm not going to live forever, Aggie. This is a dangerous line of work. I could die tomorrow. I just want to know you'll be okay if something happens to me."

She shrugged. "I guess I'll kill the son-of-a-bitch who killed you, then get on with my life. Get married, have some kids, you know..."

"I don't think you're the married-with-kids type," Roche said gently. "And I'm proud of you for it."

Aggie blushed. "I don't need a man, but that doesn't mean it wouldn't be nice to have one." She sighed. "The kids in Ojinaga used to tease me, tell me I'd be alone forever. There's a big part of me that wants to prove them wrong."

A chuckle. "I think if they could see you now, they wouldn't say that."

"Damn straight!" Aggie grinned. "You've taught me a lot, so I think I could make it on my own." She took a deep breath. "Not that I want to lose you. The first time I saw you, when I found you in that canyon where those assholes left you, I thought I'd found you and lost you in the same moment."

Now Roche smiled. "I'm glad you found me when you did."

Below them, the door to the house opened, and a group of men came out.

"Time to go to work," Aggie announced, raising her rifle and taking aim.

Chapter 2

Aggie woke to find the storm still raging outside the cave, lightning occasionally illuminating the night. She could hear the roar of water flowing down the canyon and crashing over the waterfall.

She wondered how bad the flooding would be in the valley. Would they be stuck here until the water level went down? Or would the desert ground soak it up right away?

At least Padre was good company. He hadn't pried, but Aggie had still found herself telling the story of the Screaming House and her father's death.

It felt good to tell it, almost like a form of healing, even if the hole in her heart from Roche's death was still there.

Padre had also told her more about Devil's Fork.

"It's the only town in the New Mexico Territory we're forbidden to visit," Padre said, taking a bite of his own jerky. "It's been that way for years, since before I was ordained. I asked an older priest about it years ago, and he said it's been off limits for as long as he could remember, too."

"That's strange, isn't it?" Aggie asked. "Isn't the goal to spread the gospel to as many people as possible?"

Padre shrugged. "When I was ordained, I vowed obedience to my bishop. If he tells me a place is off limits, I avoid it. Even today, if travel is possible, I only intend to pass through, not stop. We're allowed to do that, but most don't if they can help it." Padre lowered his voice conspiratorially. "I was talking to a parishioner in Santa Fe, a native, and he told me that among the tribes, Devil's Fork is known as 'The Place of the Banished.'"

"The what?"

Padre shrugged. "I don't know what he meant, and he wouldn't say more. I do know that occasionally, I've heard of people disappearing near here, but I've never seen any proof. But people disappear everywhere, strike out on their own paths without telling anyone. Without bodies, it's hard to know for certain."

If he hadn't been a priest, Aggie would have thought Padre was telling ghost stories. Hell, she still wasn't sure she believed everything he'd told her.

The sound of the rain and the rushing of the river were lulling her back to sleep when she saw a faint glow in the deepest part of the cave.

Her eyes narrowed, and she looked over at Padre. He was fast asleep.

They hadn't built a fire because all the fuel was soaked by the storm. Getting to her feet, she walked around Gato toward the glow.

She found an opening among the rocks, barely wide enough for her to fit through. At the bottom, the light was brighter, like it was coming from a tunnel of some kind.

"Everything okay?"

Padre's voice made her jump. She whirred around to find him holding up his hands.

"I'm sorry, I didn't mean to startle you."

"It's fine," Aggie said, brushing a stray hank of hair from her face. "Look at this."

The priest knelt next to the opening. "Do you hear that? It sounds like chanting."

Aggie knelt next to him, and heard a strange, rhythmic sound coming through the opening. "Religious?"

Padre shrugged. "It's not Catholic."

Aggie smiled. "That narrows it down some."

He reached inside his cassock and took out a necklace. Taking it off, he handed it to Aggie.

"What's this?" She looked at the medallion. It was vaguely familiar.

"Saint Christopher. For protection."

She smiled. Roche had found one on a body when they'd been bounty hunters. *Didn't protect him much*, Roche had observed at the time.

"Why are you giving it to me?"

Padre smiled. "You're going down there to see what's going on, aren't you? Your eyes give it away. Since I'm a little too well fed to go with you," he patted his stomach, "I'll send what help I can."

Aggie took the necklace and put it around her neck. The metal gleamed in the faint light coming from the tunnel. "Thanks."

Rocks pressed against Aggie as she crawled through the claustrophobic passage. In some spots, the opening was so narrow, she had to pull her body through, thankful she wasn't more endowed in certain places—that would make the passage impossible for her. She thought the tunnel was leading her toward the river, but she wasn't certain.

The farther she went, the brighter the light shone, and the louder the chanting got. Eventually, the passage grew wider, and finally she reached the end.

Aggie found herself on a thin ledge, looking down at a large cavern carved into the rock. Nearby, she could see a wall of water, and realized the cavern was behind the waterfall.

She peeked over the edge and gasped. Twenty feet beneath her, a massive pair of jet-black hounds lay in the corner, chewing on something. Aggie looked closer, and saw a human foot on the end of one of the dog's meals. The other one had its snout buried in a cracked-open ribcage. It lifted its head for a moment, holding some kind of organ in its powerful jaws.

Aggie didn't dare make a sound. What kind of people let a dog eat human remains? These people weren't even paying attention to the dogs; they were over at the altar, continuing their chanting.

Looking around, she saw three other holes emptying onto the ledge. What was this? Some old cave system that had been repurposed for this weird ceremony?

But why were the dogs eating human remains?

She looked down again, and one of the dogs stood, revealing it had been lying on a woman's head. The pieces scattered around the dogs were in various states of being chewed on, but the ends of the limbs showed signs of having been torn, like powerful jaws had ripped the body apart in a brutal tug-of-war.

Aggie just hoped she'd been dead when it happened.

Was she one of the people Padre had heard went missing around here?

The chanting increased in intensity, and she followed the glowing orbs of light to the far end of the chamber, where a stone altar had been built before a plain rock face. Aggie counted fifteen figures in blood-red robes and hoods marching around the altar, as other robed and hooded figures stood along the walls of the chamber, watching the ceremony.

Something had been placed in the center of the altar, on what looked like a golden plate. Aggie struggled to see it as the robed figures kept blocking her view, but then they stopped, and she got a good look.

A beating human heart lay on the plate, dark blood congealing around it.

Fort McKinney, Wyoming, two years earlier

"Are you religious, Roche?"

They were still in the infirmary at Fort McKinney, where Aggie had taken Roche after finding him left for dead. He was still recovering, but awake and alert, letting his body heal.

Roche shrugged. "I guess, maybe a little." He smiled. "Being away from your mother, I always had to believe some higher power was pulling for me."

Aggie nodded understanding. Her horizons had expanded in the two years since she'd left Ojinaga, and she was trying to figure out how what she'd learned fit into the belief system she'd always had. Roche had seen the world and been through a lot, and she found getting her father's perspective helped her figure things out.

"I have some doubts," Aggie admitted. "Some of the people in churches, they'd look down on me for some of the things I've done, that I've had to do."

Roche reached out and put his hand on top of Aggie's. "There are good people and bad people in religion, just like there's good people and bad people anywhere you go." He chuckled. "You should see some of the assholes I served with in the Army. But overall, the Army is a positive thing, just like a church. And when you find the good people, they'll understand and help you become what you're meant to be. Not just that, they'll also show you what the institution as a whole can be at its best."

Chapter 3

To Aggie's wonder and dismay, the wall behind the altar changed. Glowing carvings appeared in the rock face, ornate images and text in a language she didn't recognize. The carvings spread from the top of the wall toward the ground, the chanting getting louder and more frantic as the symbols cascaded to the cavern's rock-and-dirt floor.

Then they stopped.

The top of the wall had opened, red light from beyond it dancing along the roof of the cave. Aggie thought it looked like flames, then a sulfuric scent hit her, making her gag.

The opening looked like an arched doorway of some kind, a portal to somewhere beyond, Aggie thought.

A portal to where?

A robed figure rose in front of Aggie, floating in midair. With a red hand, it reached up and pulled its hood off.

Aggie screamed.

It was humanoid, but its skin was blood red and it had no hair. Instead, a pair of horns protruded from its scalp, curving along the thing's skull to end at its neck.

And it was looking right at her.

"Hello there," it said. "You're not supposed to be here, are you?"

Aggie scrambled backward, trying to get away, but she found herself against the rock wall of the cave. The creature approached her, rising over the ledge and reaching for her neck.

Its claw-like hand brushed against the medallion Padre had given her, and its skin burst into flames.

A scream rose from the creature's mouth, and the chanting stopped as the rest of the figures turned to look at them.

Aggie saw her chance. Pushing off from the rock, she dove for the tunnel mouth she had used to reach the cavern. Behind her, the screaming stopped, replaced by murmuring that got closer: the sounds of pursuit. Aggie clambered through the tight space, pulling herself along as fast as she could, scraping her forearms raw, ignoring the sounds of something climbing into the tunnel behind her.

She kicked a rock loose, and heard a cry of pain. She smiled in brief triumph, but then she reached a narrow point and gasped as a sharp outcropping of rock gouged her skin. But she couldn't stop—she breathed through the pain and kept moving.

She was at the top now, and Padre reached down to lift her out. As she grasped his hand, another hand grabbed her foot, trying to pull her back.

Something splashed on her face.

Water? Why was Padre throwing water?

She heard a scream from beneath her, then felt herself flying out of the hole as the thing let go of her foot. Aggie landed on the hard floor of the cave, the air whooshing from her lungs with the impact.

She raised her head and looked back. In the dim light from the tunnel, she could see Padre shaking water from a small vial down the hole. "Go!" he called to her. "I'll hold them off!"

Aggie saw the cross on the vial, and realized it was holy water. Padre was chanting prayers in Latin now, words she barely recognized from her youth. The pace and volume of the prayers increased, and Aggie knew the creatures must be getting closer.

The horses were gone. They'd probably bolted at the first signs of panic. As good a horse as Gato was, he spooked easily.

But she couldn't worry about that now.

Aggie ran out of the cave mouth. The rain had stopped, but the roar of the water soon drowned out Padre's prayers. Scrambling up the trail, she saw a crevice in the rock and slid her body into it.

Would they chase her?

A scream came from inside the cave, and Aggie fought the urge to go back and help Padre. Her guns were still in the cave. Besides, this was his fight, against demons and principalities. She wasn't sure what she could do against them. Padre was a holy man, a priest. He had it under control, she was sure of it.

Guilt hit Aggie then. She wasn't the kind to back down from a fight, no matter the odds. Padre had been a good friend. She owed it to him to try to help.

She peeked out of her hiding spot and gasped.

Hooded figures were coming up the trail now, shadows in the dark, moonless night. They gathered around the cave entrance, chanting in the language from before, their voices rising over the thunder of the water and echoing off the canyon walls. Aggie tried to count, but it was difficult in the darkness. She gave up when she realized the number was at least a dozen.

New plan.

She couldn't help Padre if she was captured by these demon-things too.

Aggie watched as three of them went into the cave.

The chanting continued. Aggie waited, hoping to hear more screaming, signs that Padre was defeating these bastards.

Instead, the figures outside the cave cleared a path, and the chanting became more frantic.

Hooded figures came out of the cave.

Then Aggie saw Padre, floating vertically behind them, following the hooded creatures.

The chanting was louder now, at a fever pitch, and Aggie realized she could understand it.

We have a holy one,

A new hope to opening the portal.

When the full moon comes,

This world will unite with our home

And destruction will reign

As the harvest begins

And the Prince of Darkness rises!

Aggie crept down the trail after the robed figures, careful not to make a sound as she watched them descend. When they reached the bottom, they floated over the water, disappearing through the waterfall.

What the fuck had they meant by the Prince of Darkness? Uniting worlds at the full moon? It sounded like they expected the fucking devil to break out of their portal.

She remembered the fire and sulfur smell in the cave, and gasped.

That's exactly what they meant to do.

The devil was going to break out of the portal.

Fucking Hell.

There had to be a way to stop it.

She climbed back to the cave to find the contents of the saddlebags scattered around. Her gun belt was wedged behind a rock, and though the leather was scuffed, the weapon was in good shape. Aggie strapped it on before returning her bedroll to the cave wall and leaning against it.

Alone, Aggie started second-guessing herself. She should have taken a weapon down into the tunnel with her, something more powerful than a stupid medallion.

She closed her eyes, remembering her derringer was still tucked behind her belt.

Fuck.

But would it have mattered? Could these beasts, these demons, be killed by mere bullets? Aggie didn't know.

All Aggie was sure of was that she was bad news for men. First Roche, and now Padre had suffered because of her.

Roche wasn't your fault, a voice in her head reassured her.

The fuck he wasn't. If she'd been faster, more brutal, she might have saved him.

You did what he taught you, the voice came again. *You took down almost a dozen men trying to save him!*

But it hadn't worked.

And now, demons had Padre, the only friend she'd found since her father's death.

Something glistened on the ground, and Aggie picked it up. It was a cross necklace, the gold cross surrounded by red emeralds. Maybe Padre's? She put it in her pocket, figuring if the demons didn't like Saint Christopher or holy water, a cross would also help against them.

Padre's words drifted back to her: "The Place of the Banished," Devil's Fork. What if the banished were demons, imprisoned in the town and trying to escape? It seemed possible, even likely now.

But if she was going to know for sure, she'd have to pay Devil's Fork a visit.

Durango, Colorado, five months earlier

"Why didn't you look for someone else when you got Abuelo's letter?" Aggie asked, poking at the campfire with a stick. "You weren't old or anything. You could have gotten married, had a new family."

She'd learned a lot about her father in the two years since she'd found him, but that was one of the few questions she'd never gotten around to asking. Roche and her mother, Ysidra had met when he was stationed at Fort Davis, Texas; and when Aggie's grandfather had discovered the relationship, he'd taken Ysidra back to their hometown of Ojinaga.

By then, Roche's seed had taken root, and nine months later, Aggie was born. Her angry grandfather had returned to Fort Davis, only to find that the Civil War had broken out and Roche, a northerner, had returned home to fight for the Union. When the war ended, her grandfather sent Roche a letter via the War Department, telling him Ysidra had found someone else and didn't want anything to do with him.

A lie. But it had kept Roche away until Aggie found him and told him the truth.

"I never found anyone I loved as much as I loved your mother," Roche said. "There have been beautiful women, wonderful women, who I've met since your grandfather forced us apart. But none has been your mother. And if I couldn't have something better, I wasn't going to settle for less."

"So you're just an old romantic, that's your problem?" Aggie asked with a smile.

"Something like that." Roche smiled too. "Did you ask your mother the same question?"

Aggie nodded. "She said to get to her, someone was going to have to whip Abuelo's ass, and after what he did to you, she figured it was reserved for you."

Roche laughed. "God, that does sound like her. The Ysidra I saw when we were together, not the subdued, shrinking violet she was around your grandfather."

"How did you manage to see her without my grandfather finding out?" Aggie asked.

"We had a special place at a nearby creek. Your grandfather was gone for long periods of time on his trips, so while your grandmother, who was bedridden, rested, Ysidra and I would get together."

"I ain't innocent. You can say what you were doing," Aggie said with a grin.

Roche laughed. "There was some of that, but it was more than that. I can't really explain it. Someday, you'll find someone and know exactly what I'm talking about. You just like being around them, it doesn't matter what you're doing."

"And you really like doing certain things with them," Aggie teased.

Roche nodded. "That's true too."

CHAPTER 4

Aggie woke to find sunlight streaming through the cave's entrance.

She hadn't meant to sleep. Her back had been to the cave entrance, one eye on the hole at the rear of the cave, listening to the sounds of celebration that drifted up from the creatures' chamber, waiting for them to return for her.

But they never came. The only sign the demons were still down there was chanting, the same chant they'd celebrated Padre's capture with.

Maybe that was it. They didn't care about her because they had the one they needed: Padre.

She needed to do something, anything, to rescue him before the full moon. But first she had to get herself out of this mess.

The horses still hadn't come back. Aggie figured they were farther up the canyon somewhere. Her own provisions and supplies were scattered around her, the saddlebags flung against the wall. Padre's belongings had received the same treatment. She had been able to recover some jerky, but most of her other food, flour and similar staples, had been scattered among the dirt and rocks on the cave floor.

Aggie couldn't help but wonder why they'd done that. They had Padre. Why'd they need to trash the supplies? There wasn't a good reason for that.

Or maybe there was.

Because now she had no choice but to stop in Devil's Fork to resupply.

Maybe the demons were smarter than she gave them credit for. The last trading post she'd seen on her ride in was twenty miles behind her. That'd be a hell of a long walk in the sun. Devil's Fork was only a few miles away, but she'd still arrive exhausted—easy prey for anyone who wanted to take advantage of her.

But if the demons she saw last night were in Devil's Fork, how had no one seen them before now? How come no one spoke of Devil's Fork in hushed tones, talking about the murderous creatures that lurked there? The owner of the trading post had sent her toward the town without hesitation or apparent guile.

But now she knew better.

She'd wait for nightfall and try to approach unnoticed, then see what she could discover.

Aggie spent the rest of the day looking for more chimneys. She found a likely one farther up the river, concealed under an overhang. It was an almost-vertical drop into the darkness, requiring a rope to aid any decent or ascent.

She'd considered returning to the cavern through her original chimney, trying to see if Padre was still there and what she could expect, but even though the demons hadn't come back for her yet, she couldn't escape the feeling they'd be watching for her.

If she didn't turn up for a day or two, they'd probably assume she'd left town, or perhaps died in the wilderness.

She hoped so, anyway.

As the sun set over the western wall of the canyon, she slipped down the trail next to the waterfall, trying to move as silently and as stealthily as she could.

Out on the plains, she encountered her first crisis: hoofbeats on the trail ahead of her. Aggie slipped behind a pile of rocks. Peeking over the top, she saw two mounted figures riding toward the falls.

"Damn guard duty. It's fucking bullshit!"

Aggie thought it would be a demon, but as the rider approached, she realized it looked like a man.

"It's just until we're sure that other one is gone," the second rider replied. "If you'd grabbed her like you should have, we wouldn't have to worry about it."

"I would have killed her if it wasn't for that damn medallion she was wearing," the first man growled.

The moon came out, and she saw splotches on the rider's pale skin.

From the holy water, Aggie thought. *But he looks like a man now…*

As the riders passed, she noticed a bandage on the scarred man's hand. Fingering the medallion Padre had given her, she couldn't help but smile. He thought he would have killed her, huh? Too bad she forgot about her derringer… She'd have shown him a thing or two before she ran.

As they rode out of sight, she started to emerge from her hiding place, but then she realized if they were going out to replace guards that were already there, those guards would be riding back to town.

She squatted back down, flattening herself against the rocks.

Soon, she heard hoofbeats coming from the direction of the falls.

"Why couldn't they put the portal closer to town," a voice griped. "We could fly out in a minute."

"Because then folks would see our true forms."

"Hell, they'll see them soon enough."

Both riders laughed.

"Pretending to be human is exhausting," the first rider said.

"But worth it!" his friend replied. "I've never consumed better!"

"And we had to get exorcized for it!"

Exorcized? Aggie thought. *What the fuck is going on around here?*

The laughter continued as the demons rode toward town. As soon as they had disappeared in the darkness, Aggie crept out from her hiding place and followed them.

A dusty collection of buildings appeared on the horizon, and Aggie slipped off the trail to approach through the scrub. Moving behind the buildings, she heard laughter coming from one of them.

Probably the saloon, she decided. As good a place to start her research as any.

Saloons were one of the first places she and Roche stopped when they arrived in a new town in pursuit of a fugitive. They were full of information and rumors, and occasionally they'd even find the people they were looking for sitting right at the bar, already half drunk and easy to grab.

But even though the only resident of Devil's Fork who would recognize her was on guard duty, she still wanted to be discreet.

Approaching the back door, she shimmied up a drainpipe to an open window. Aggie peeked inside to see a young woman tied to a bed. The rope had started to chafe, leaving her wrists and ankles red and raw. A shirt had been stuffed in her mouth, the sleeves tied around the back of her head to hold it in place.

When she was working as a prostitute, Aggie had entertained clients with peculiar tastes like this. But she knew this was different.

The girl tied to the bed looked terrified.

A bone saw and scalpel were sitting on the nightstand. Aggie noticed the bed was tilted, with thin railings along the side and a bucket waiting at the foot. There wasn't even a mattress under the woman, just a sheet of metal.

This wasn't a bordello.

It was something much worse.

South of Boise, Idaho, three months earlier

Aggie and Roche were hiding in a cave. On the plains below, they could see the outlaw gang searching for them.

"What do we do?" Aggie asked.

"We stay here, wait for them to think we've run away."

Aggie raised an eyebrow. "You think running away is the best option."

Roche shook his head. "No, and I didn't say that. I said we want them to think we've run away. Then they won't be looking for us, and we can make our move."

Aggie nodded her understanding. "I don't like waiting," she admitted.

Roche grinned. "I didn't either, when I was your age. Especially when I was waiting for your mother."

"She hasn't enjoyed waiting for you all these years, I can promise that."

A nod.

That was something that pissed her off about her father. When she was angry, he was stoic, not letting his emotions show.

"I hate that I've kept her waiting." Roche sighed. "A few more jobs, then we'll head for Ojinaga, and I'll never leave her again."

Chapter 5

Aggie jumped to the windowsill and pulled herself inside.

When the woman tied to the bed saw Aggie, her eyes went wide and she shook her head. Aggie walked over and untied the sleeves before pulling the gag out of her mouth.

"You've got to get out of here," the woman whispered. "He'll be here soon."

"Who will?" Aggie asked.

"Dewey." The woman swallowed, glancing at the door. "He's going to consume me."

"All the more reason to get you out of here," Aggie said, reaching for one of the ropes binding the woman.

"No, you don't understand. There's no escape, not from the hounds. They'll run me down."

Aggie stopped. "The hounds?"

A nod. "The hounds of hell. I saw a man, Casey Brewer, who tried to run for Santa Fe. The hounds drug him back, covered in blood and screaming. They're as big as bears, mean as rattlesnakes, and smart as hell."

Aggie raised an eyebrow. "Is that a joke?"

She shook her head. "Ain't no joke. I've never seen dogs like them, and my pa had a champion pack back in Mississippi. After those monster dogs drug Casey back, Wilmore left him alive while he consumed his soul, right there in the street, then let the dogs have what was left." She shuddered. "Ain't never heard screaming like that, especially from a man with no soul. I didn't expect he'd be able to feel anything, but then I learned. If they want you to hurt, you will."

Aggie sat down on the edge of the bed. "You said this Wilmore guy consumed him?"

"You know they're demons, right?"

Aggie nodded.

"They put us mortals to work—some more willing, like me, and some not, like Casey Brewer—and when one of them gets hungry, they choose one of us to consume." Her body shuddered again. "I've had to clean my share of rooms after consumption. They're not neat creatures. There's always blood everywhere."

"But the soul? It's not attached to your body, right?" Aggie's religious education hadn't been formal or thorough, but she was sure of that much.

"That's part of their power," the woman explained. "They bind your soul to your heart, then crack your chest and dig in." She jerked her head toward the tools on the nightstand. "Most don't even bother to use those. They rip you open with their bare hands. And if you piss them off? They'll make sure you scream; the sound of you hurting makes it better for them. Adds to the excitement."

"But how did you end up here? Did they kidnap you?" Aggie shook her head. "I'm sorry, I haven't even asked your name."

"Martha." A smile. "And I came looking for work, just like anyone. Another new town, another new start. Except this is the end of the line." She looked at the door again. "You should go, before Dewey comes and finds you."

Aggie put a hand on hers. "Not without you."

Martha shook her head. "I'm scared of the dogs. I'd rather go this way, and die with what little dignity I have left."

"That's ridiculous!" Aggie blurted out.

"It's my choice!" Martha replied. "That's something else I forgot to mention. Everyone who ends up as a slave in Devil's Fork does it by choice, by agreement. Most of the men are gamblers, who put their souls on the line in wagers downstairs."

"What about you?" Aggie asked.

She sighed. "I've worked as a soiled dove ever since I ran away from home when I was sixteen. It hasn't been all bad, but something happened in the last town." Martha lifted her body off the bed, showing Aggie her back.

Aggie gasped. A network of scars crisscrossed the flesh. It looked painful, and from the way some seemed to be more healed than others, it looked like they'd happened over a period of months, if not years.

"Las Vegas, New Mexico," Martha said. "Big Stan Holloway made me his personal woman, gave me an allowance and everything. I thought I was set, until the beatings started. He had some strange tastes. I bet you've never seen anything like it."

"You'd be surprised," Aggie said, thinking back to what she'd seen in the Screaming House. That brought Roche to her mind, and she felt a tear forming. Shaking her head to push the emotion away, she focused on Martha's face. "But you thought being here, getting consumed, would be better than that?"

"I didn't know I was going to be consumed. The demons told me in exchange for my soul, they'd make sure no man laid his hand on me again. I figured with what I'd done, I'm already damned to hell. Might as well get something good out of it. But that contract didn't specify when they got my soul, and I didn't think to ask."

"So they decided now?"

Martha nodded. "The demons know how to get humans to make deals with them. No matter what you do, never make a deal with a demon. They'll always cheat. You have to willingly put your soul on the line before they can consume it." She sighed. "I didn't learn that until after I made my deal."

"But... We'll go to the sheriff! Something! This isn't legal, you can't just give up!"

Martha smiled. "I'm not giving up, I'm just allowing myself the dignity to make my own final decisions, and if I don't fight them—if I behave—they'll do it so it doesn't even hurt. But if you want to talk to the sheriff, stay a few minutes. Dewey will be right up."

A wave of realization washed over Aggie. "There really isn't a way out, is there?"

Martha shook her head. "But thank you for trying. It's been a while since someone cared."

Footsteps sounded in the hall outside the door.

"Go. Now."

Aggie leaned over and kissed Martha on the forehead before swinging out the window. She heard the door slam open, and peeked back inside the window.

Dewey was huge, filling the door in his human form. He threw his black cowboy hat onto a chair, revealing a head of gray hair. If Aggie'd seen him out somewhere, she'd have called him ugly. His face looked like he'd been kicked by a horse, more than once.

"I heard voices," he said, his own voice a low, rumbling growl.

"I was praying," Martha replied.

Dewey laughed, the booming rumble seeming to shake the whole building. "It's too late for that." His black eyes sparkled as he looked down at the feast awaiting him. "Much too late."

He held his hands over Martha's body, whispering words Aggie couldn't hear. Orange light lifted from her, forming a glowing ball beneath Dewey's hands. When the last bit of light was gathered, he seemed to push it down, through Martha's skin and into her chest.

Aggie stole a look at Martha's face. It was peaceful and unmoving. She was gone, her spirit brought into the orb of light she'd seen.

Dewey was smiling, looking down at the body. Raising a finger, it briefly transformed into a pointed claw. He drew it the length of Martha's torso, splitting her clothes and leaving a red line down her skin. Peeling her clothes away, he looked down at the body with a small smile, anticipation and hunger reflecting in his eyes.

Then he turned both hands into claws. Placing them on the red line he drew earlier, he pushed them into her flesh, then with a grunt pulled them apart.

Martha's ribcage broke open with a crack, the dark blood standing out even against the red skin of Dewey's hands.

He scooped something out of the bloody cavity, lifting it up. Aggie saw it was Martha's heart, a faint orange glow surrounding it.

With a smile, Dewey sank his teeth into it, blood splattering onto his face as he chewed.

It took everything in Aggie's power not to scream.

Laramie, Wyoming, two years earlier

"You think that ghost shit's real?" Aggie asked, nodding toward the book in his hands.

He shrugged. "You should hear some of the Native stories. They talk about beasts and creatures stranger than anything we've ever considered."

"And you think they're true?" Aggie pressed.

"I think everything, all stories, are born from truth," Roche said. "Or what someone believes is true. My parents were devout Lutherans, firm in their faith, not the type to believe in ghosts or anything like that. But when I open my bible and it falls on one of my mother's favorite passages, it's easy to believe her spirit had a hand in it. Even if a ghostly hand doesn't appear to stop the pages."

"What about the creatures the Natives talked about?"

He shrugged. "If you've ever been alone at night somewhere outdoors, everything seems bigger and scarier. Maybe some things do hide in the dark that we want to pretend aren't real. I don't know."

"So are you saying you believe in that kind of stuff?" Aggie asked. "So far you've done everything but answer the question."

Roche laughed. "That used to annoy your mother, too. She said I had to argue with myself before I gave her an answer."

"Damn it, Roche," Aggie growled. "Give me an answer, or I'm gonna undo all the healing you've done in the last six months."

"Maybe," he said, grinning. "If a ghost, or a demon, or another strange creature popped up in front of me, I wouldn't be so surprised I couldn't react."

Chapter 6

Aggie had felt her own heart racing as she fought the urge to look away, to retreat down the drainpipe and disappear into the night. This had to be stopped. No more devouring, no more deals, no more demons.

When Dewey left the room, she slid down the drainpipe and found a hiding place behind some barrels.

She needed a horse.

She needed food.

She needed a lot of things.

But a horse was the most pressing need.

With a horse, she could ride farther down the valley to Espanola, out of reach of the demons and their nonsense. Maybe she could even make it to Santa Fe, where the bishop would surely be interested in Padre's fate.

But first, she needed a horse.

The rider dismounted in front of the saloon. Aggie had been watching him since he appeared at the edge of town. From the way he turned his head, looking at the buildings, she guessed he wasn't a local.

Aggie saw a bulging money belt as he swung off the horse, marking him as a gambler.

If what Martha told her was true, Aggie doubted he would be needing his horse.

A priest, maybe, but not his horse.

She waited until he'd gone inside the saloon, then peeked in a window and saw him heading toward the gambling table at the back, where a poker game was in progress.

Perfect.

Emerging from the shadows, she walked to the rail and untied the horse's reins. Up close, she could see it was a bay, a little smaller than Gato. It whinnied when Aggie tried to lead it away, so she got close and whispered.

"Look, I know I'm not your owner, but this is an emergency!"

It snorted, but let her slowly lead it away from the saloon. Aggie walked the horse to the edge of town, then swung into the saddle and rode south.

Her heart was pounding, and Aggie was sure everyone in town could hear it. No matter what happened to the horse's owner in Devil's Fork, this was still horse theft, a hanging offense. Though in Devil's Fork, she doubted she'd face a walk to the gallows.

They'd probably just rip her in two and eat her heart.

When the town had faded to a speck of light on the horizon behind her, she spurred the horse into a run. The three-quarter moon was bright enough to see the trail ahead, and she wanted to be as far from Devil's Fork as possible when her theft was discovered.

Was it only a couple months ago she'd been riding like this with her papa, escaping the Briar Hill jail but falling right into Ray Spencer's trap?

She shook her head to clear it. God, she didn't need to think about that right now.

It was time to find help.

Miles passed at a run, and Aggie splashed across a pair of creeks. The horse had good stamina, she realized.

Maybe the gambler was crooked, and needed a good horse to get out of town in a hurry.

Whatever the reason, she silently thanked him for it.

But then the horse stumbled, its front legs collapsing under it and sending Aggie over its head onto the road. She bounced on her ass once, twice, three times before skidding to a stop.

Getting to her feet, she took mental inventory of her condition.

Her legs worked.

Her arms worked.

Her head felt okay.

Her ass... She winced. Not a lot of cushioning back there, but she'd be fine.

Then she heard the horse.

It was braying loudly, its cries filled with pain. Walking back to where it lay fallen, Aggie saw its front leg bent at an unnatural angle.

Fuck. The leg was broken.

Pulling out her pistol, Aggie pressed it to the horse's head and squeezed the trigger.

The muffled sound of the gunshot hurt Aggie almost as much as the fall had. The horse had been good to her, taken her far from the demons in Devil's Fork, but with a broken leg, she had to do it, to end the animal's suffering.

Turning back to the south, Aggie began walking.

She'd been walking about an hour when she saw the glow of a fire on the horizon.

Soon enough, she reached the camp and saw the man sitting by the fire.

The first thing she noticed was the long brown robe, tied at the waist with a length of rope. A simple wooden cross hung around his neck, and above it, Aggie was surprised to find a youthful face with bright blue eyes and brown hair.

"Hello," the monk greeted her.

"Hello," Aggie replied. He was handsome, but she knew the robe meant he was unavailable.

Damn it.

Aggie didn't usually want sex; spending time working in whorehouses to gather information as a bounty hunter had given her more than she needed, but something about running from demons and the hounds of hell was igniting that flame.

"What are you doing out here?" the monk asked.

She smiled. "You probably wouldn't believe me if I told you."

A gentle smile. "It's possible. But I do like a good story, especially at bedtime."

Aggie sighed. "There's a town populated by demons about ten miles behind me. I'm trying to get to Espanola, or maybe Santa Fe, to report they've captured a priest."

The monk's smile disappeared. "How d'you know that?"

"I was there when they took him."

He got to his feet, walking around the fire. "And they let you go?"

"I was hiding. We found their temple by accident. They saw me, and chased me to where Padre and I were waiting out a storm." A tear rolled down Aggie's cheek. "Padre told me to run, that he would hold them off."

The monk reached out and grabbed a handful of Aggie's shirt. "You expect me to believe your lies, demon?"

Aggie didn't realize her fist was swinging until it hit the monk's cheek. He let go of her and stumbled backward. "You punched me!"

"You called me a demon!" she shot back.

"What am I supposed to think? You show up looking like a temptation shot straight from Satan's quiver, telling a story about Padre, and I'm supposed to believe you?" His hand covered the spot where she'd hit him. "Saints, you pack a wallop!"

"Grab me like that again, and you can have another!" Aggie shook her head. "I'm not a demon, damn you! I'm just an unfortunate soul who found herself in a hell of a pickle!"

"Prove it!"

"Prove what?"

"That you're not a demon!"

How the hell was she supposed to do that? Aggie remembered the cave, the demon reaching for her neck, then falling away, screaming.

Padre's medallion.

She undid the top two buttons on her shirt, and saw the monk cover his eyes and look away. "Stop that, you idiot. I'm not going to tempt you." Aggie pulled out the medallion and held it up. "If I were a demon, could I wear this?"

The monk stepped toward her and reached out, taking the pendant in his fingers. "Padre," he whispered, his face pale except for the bruise forming where Aggie had punched him. "I guess you're not a liar."

"No, but she is a horse thief…"

Chapter 7

Aggie cringed as Sheriff Dewey stepped into the firelight, leading a tall, black horse that reminded her of Gato. He was still in his human form, and she could still see the blood on his shirt and in his beard from when he had consumed Martha.

She wanted to kill him, to rip his chest open the way he had Martha's and tear his beating heart out with her bare hands.

"Seems someone stopped in Devil's Fork and got their horse stolen," the sheriff said. "I found a dead horse about three miles back, but no rider." He looked between Aggie and the monk before settling on Aggie. "Since he's a man of the cloth, I'm guessing you're the horse thief."

"Prove it," Aggie shot back.

"Um, Sheriff," the Monk cut in. "My name is Brother Gabriel, and I'm happy to vouch for this woman."

"Oh really?" The sheriff turned toward him. "Are you the horse thief?"

Gabriel shook his head. "We haven't seen a horse thief, have we?"

Aggie shook her head, wondering if the monk's innocence might get them out of this.

The sheriff stepped closer to the monk, towering over him. "What's her name?"

"What?" The monk looked helpless.

"What's her name."

The monk looked at Aggie, then back at the sheriff.

"That's what I thought." The sheriff turned toward Aggie, who had moved to stand next to Brother Gabriel's horse. "You're a horse thief, and you're the spy who was watching our ceremony the other day. That damn priest may have saved you once, but he'll never know what happens out here..."

The contents of the vial hit the sheriff in the face, and he stumbled backward, screaming, landing ass-first in the glowing coals of the fire. He tried to roll away, but his clothes had caught.

"What did you do?" Brother Gabriel shouted, staring in horror.

"Borrowed some holy water!" Burns were appearing where the fluid had landed on the demon's face, and his eyes were red and swollen.

Aggie reached in her pocket and pulled out Padre's cross. Kneeling next to the thrashing demon, she pressed the cross into his chest. The screaming got louder as the sheriff convulsed and twisted, but Aggie held the cross there until it was absorbed into the demon's skin.

She jumped back as the hands that had been clawing at the demon's face moved to his chest. Claws replaced his fingers as Dewey returned to his true form, slashing into his own skin, trying to reach the cross.

"What is that?" Brother Gabriel asked.

Aggie looked down as the demon sheriff's scream faded away, his blank eyes staring up at the sky. "A dead demon."

"What? A demon? But he's the sheriff?"

She turned, fire glowing in her eyes. "Yes. The demon sheriff of a demon town. And he was going to try to kill us!"

The monk's jaw dropped. "*Us?* But *I* didn't do anything! You're the horse thief!"

Aggie rolled her eyes. "You think that matters? We're not important to him, we're just food to consume! Earlier tonight, I saw him tear a woman apart and eat her soul!"

"Lord have mercy. And he's the *law*?"

"Yes! Which means the law is what he wants it to be!" Aggie reached into the demon's chest and pulled out Padre's pendant, covered in a black substance she assumed was the demon's blood. "Here," she held it out to Gabriel. "This may come in handy again."

Gabriel held it between two fingers. "That's gross."

Aggie rolled her eyes again. "You need to get out of the monastery more."

The sun was rising when they finished dragging the sheriff's body into a nearby draw. Vultures were already circling overhead, and Aggie had a feeling they'd make quick work of the scorched remains.

She wondered if demon meat tasted any different from everything else the winged scavengers ate.

"So how'd a greenhorn like you get sent on a rescue mission?" she asked Gabriel.

He bowed his head. "They actually didn't send me. The abbot forbade me from coming, but I disobeyed him. I'm going to be in so much trouble when I get back."

"So why'd you come?' Aggie asked.

"Padre is like a father to me," he explained. "He brought me out of the orphanage, and practically raised me there in the monastery. When the demons sent the message they had him, bragging about it, I knew I had to do something." Gabriel bowed his head. "Though now, I think I might be in over my head."

Aggie put her hand on his shoulder. "Don't worry. We'll get Padre back."

"I don't see how," Gabriel said.

A smile. "Isn't there a bible story about a man who killed a bunch of people with the jawbone of an ass?"

Gabriel looked up, a small smile on his face. "Samson?"

Aggie nodded. "Well, I ain't got the jawbone of an ass, but I know how to whoop some ass."

Helena, Montana, a year earlier

"You ever think about when you were a greenhorn?" Aggie asked.

Roche took a sip of his whiskey. The bar was nearly empty, the two of them at the end opposite where the barman was working. "All the time. I thought I knew everything, but I didn't know shit." He smiled. "Took me a few days to figure out I wasn't as smart as I thought I was."

"Days?" Aggie said.

Roche laughed. "War teaches you real quick, Aggie. The first time I saw an Apache, I froze. I just stood there, him running right at me. My sergeant grabbed me, threw me to the ground, and it snapped me out of it. Had to do the same thing to a lot of kids during the war. You can train folks all you want, but the first time you see an actual enemy, feel an actual bullet whistle by? That's the kind of lesson you don't forget."

Aggie nodded. "Sometimes I wonder if I could handle being responsible for a greenhorn."

"You're still a damn greenhorn yourself," Roche said, taking another sip of his whiskey. "But when the time comes, you'll figure it out."

"You think?" Aggie asked.

"Of course." He finished his whiskey, then sat the glass on the bar and smiled. "Of course, your first greenhorn might not survive, but there'll be more..."

CHAPTER 8

Whatever Aggie had been expecting, watching Gabriel try to ride a horse was worse than she had imagined. Her laughter didn't help.

By the time they reached the dead horse, he'd fallen out of the saddle more times than she could count. His robe meant he had to ride sidesaddle, and he wasn't very good at staying upright.

Aggie was beginning to wonder if joining forces with him was a mistake. But at the same time, she felt obligated to help him, because he sure as shit wouldn't survive the demons on his own.

"So why are the demons here anyway," Aggie asked, trying to save him from embarrassment after another fall. She was on the sheriff's horse, a spirited black morgan that had tried to bite her the first time she'd climbed on. Then it had bucked, dropping its head and kicking in a display that left Gabriel open mouthed, but Aggie had hung on, and the horse decided against wasting any more energy fighting her.

"Exorcisms," Gabriel said, lifting himself back into the saddle. "When the priest banishes them, they have to go somewhere, and an isolated place like this is as good as any."

Aggie reined her horse in. "Not hell?"

Gabriel shook his head. "You think an exorcised demon wants to go back and face the devil? They begged the bishop to give them a place like this so they didn't have to face Lucifer right after an exorcism."

"So it's the church's fault the demons are out here?"

He shrugged. "Would you rather they be wandering the earth, possessing folks?"

She thought for a minute. "Well, no, but a warning would have been nice. 'Demons ahead, go the other way.'"

Gabriel shook his head. "It's part of the agreement. They stay in Devil's Fork, the church doesn't warn people about them. Demons have to eat, too. The bishop who made the agreement figured it was better to have them all in one place, and let anyone unlucky enough to find it fend for themselves."

"How come Padre didn't know this?" Aggie asked. "All he said was he wasn't supposed to stay in Devil's Fork."

Gabriel shrugged, and slipped out of the saddle again. "As far as I know, only the bishop and a few others know the truth. I found out because the monk in the cell next to mine works in the bishop's office, and I stole his journal when I heard Padre was missing. I knew he'd know why I wasn't allowed to launch a rescue mission."

Aggie shook her head. "You must really love Padre, disobeying the abbot and stealing a journal."

"I'm just doing what I think he'd do if the roles were reversed."

Aggie had to smile at this. Though she'd only known Padre a few hours, she knew Gabriel was exactly right. If the shoe was on the other foot, Padre would be working to save him.

"So how are you planning to fight these demons?" she asked. "Did you bring a gun?"

He shook his head. "I've got holy water, a crucifix, blessed oils, a bible, and some dynamite."

"Dynamite?" Aggie raised her eyebrows. "Why would you grab all that religious shit and decide, 'You know, maybe I'll grab some dynamite, just in case...'"

Gabriel laughed. "One of the local workmen stopped me as I was leaving the monastery. He'd heard about Padre, and wanted to contribute. He didn't have much, but he had three sticks of dynamite left over from a mining job he worked, and he hoped it would help in some way."

Aggie laughed. "You going to blow the demons back to hell?"

Another shrug. "I hadn't thought that far ahead."

Aggie's smile disappeared. "Well, it's time to start thinking. If we're going to pull this off, we have to be a step ahead of these demons, or we'll end up just like Padre."

Aggie and Gabriel rode into Devil's Fork around noon. The sheriff's horse drew looks from folks on the boardwalks, but Aggie refused to meet their gazes.

When they reached the saloon, a demon-man in all black stepped into the street in front of them. In his hands, he held the leashes of the two hell hounds Aggie had seen eating the woman's body in the cavern.

"Where's the sheriff?" he asked.

"Dead. Ain't sure what happened, but it wasn't pretty," Aggie explained, watching the hounds. Their teeth were bared, both ignoring Gabriel to stare at Aggie on the sheriff's horse.

They'd agreed Aggie would be the one to do the talking. For a greenhorn, at least Gabriel knew he was in over his head. But he looked awfully nervous, staring at the massive dogs. Aggie was afraid he might blurt something out without meaning to, and that would get them both in trouble.

The man in black frowned. "You're saying something killed the sheriff?"

Aggie nodded. "We saw his body a few miles back, and found his horse wandering. Lucky thing, too. My horse had to be put down. Broken leg."

Roche had taught her the best way to tell a lie was to tell as much of the truth as you could.

The less fiction you have to remember, the better off you are.

Her father's voice echoed in her head as the man in black studied her. Then he jerked his head at Gabriel. "Why are you riding with a monk?"

"We've come to see about the priest you captured."

A shake of the head. "Can't help you there. We caught him, fair and square, and that means we can do what we want with him."

"To his body," Gabriel cut in, earning a glare from Aggie. "You can torture him, you can kill him, but you can't have his soul."

The man in black smiled. "Normally, you'd be right. But we've got our reasons for wanting all of him, and he made a special deal with us to make it possible."

Aggie remembered what Martha had said about making deals with demons, and knew it couldn't be good. "We want to see him," she said.

The man in black studied them for a moment. "It might be possible. But to allow that would be risky for us." A smile. "You'd have to risk something in return."

"What?"

Damn it, Gabriel! Aggie wanted to grab him and hold his mouth closed. Instead, she looked at him and shook her head, only for him to look away.

"Your soul?" The demon turned to Gabriel. "Wager your soul in a hand of faro, or maybe poker?"

"Deal," Gabriel said before Aggie could stop him.

"One condition," Aggie cut in as the demon passed the hounds' leashes to another demon-man and went to shake Gabriel's outstretched hand. "I'm the dealer."

The man in black paused.

"What's the matter?" Aggie asked. "Your deck, his dealer, that seems fair."

A nod. "Indeed." Grabbing Gabriel's hand, the man in black shook it.

Bozeman, Montana, a year earlier

"Put your hands up!" Roche raised his hands, and Aggie heard him cursing at being caught off guard. He'd just excused himself to step into the outhouse for a moment, but apparently it was long enough for this piece of shit to catch up to him while Aggie was hung up at the bar.

"I heard you was looking for me," the outlaw growled.

"That's right," her father said. "You've got a bounty on your head."

"Is that a fact?" The man cocked his gun. "Too bad you won't live to collect it."

Another gun cocked, this one hers. "That poster said dead or alive," Aggie explained. "And I ain't picky about which."

The outlaw let his gun fall to the ground. "Where the fuck did you come from?"

"I've been watching you all night. You watched Roche, waiting for your chance to get him alone. I watched you."

A shake of the head. "You two are something else, you know that? Ain't no other bounty hunter rides with a woman."

Roche shrugged, then picked up the outlaw's gun. "It's a family business. I gotta work with what I got."

CHAPTER 9

The saloon's main floor was a long, low room with a bar along the wall. In the corner, Aggie could see a stairway leading up to the rooms where she'd met Martha.

Every eye watched as their procession entered and made their way to one of the poker tables in the back.

"Get up, Zeke," the man in black ordered a scrawny creature sitting at the table.

"Shit, Burke, give me a minute," Zeke replied, eyeing the pot on the table.

Burke looked down at Zeke's hand. "You ain't doing shit with a nine-high. Now all of you git!"

Grumbling, Zeke and the other gamblers got to their feet. Burke and Gabriel sat down, Aggie taking a seat across from them and picking up the deck of cards from the table.

"Eli! Whiskey!" Burke yelled to the barman. Aggie saw a chain around his neck, connected to an anchor at the end of the bar. Grabbing three glasses and a bottle, he shuffled through the crowd of demons, the chain clinking on the floor behind him. It stretched just long enough for him to set the glasses on the table, then pour amber liquid into them.

"A toast!" Burke took a glass and raised it. "You should never gamble without a shot or two to steady your nerves."

Aggie took a glass from the table. Gabriel stared at the last one, then finally reached for it.

"To gambling!" Burke said, downing his glass.

Aggie tilted hers back, feeling the warmth as the whiskey burned down her throat to her stomach.

Across the table, Gabriel's hands went to his throat as he choked on the harsh liquor. Eli slapped his back and the sound ceased, leaving Gabriel with watering eyes.

"Careful now," Burke said. "Don't go losing the stake before we can settle our bet." He looked at Aggie. "Ready?"

She nodded.

Aggie knew how to shuffle, but the cards kept slipping from her hands. How dare Gabriel put his soul on the line after he'd agreed to keep his mouth shut!

"You need a minute?" Burke asked with a menacing grin. "I ain't in no hurry."

A crowd gathered around them. Aggie figured they were all demons, because none of them had chains around their necks.

Aggie took a deep breath and shook her head. "I've got this."

Using her thumbs, she rippled the cards together once, twice, three times. Cutting the deck, she picked it up.

"Draw poker, deal 'em face up," Burke said. "No need to keep us in suspense."

He rapped the table twice, and Aggie felt the cards jump in her hand.

Nerves?

It had to be.

Burke was on her left, so she dealt to him after discarding a burn. His first card was the three of clubs.

Gabriel came next. The two of hearts.

Back to Burke. Six of hearts.

Gabriel. Two of spades.

Burke. Five of diamonds.

Gabriel. Ace of hearts.

"You know," Burke said with a grin, staring across the table at Aggie. "We could make this more interesting. Want to put your soul on the line, too?"

Aggie shook her head. "Not a damn chance."

Burke shrugged.

Looking around, Aggie saw something in the eyes of the crowd. Not curiosity, but anticipation, as if they knew what was going to happen, a liturgy that had played out hundreds if not thousands of times before.

There was a fix in.

Aggie flipped the next card and laid it in front of Burke. The seven of clubs. He smiled, and she flipped the next card. The two of clubs went in front of Gabriel.

He breathed a sigh of relief, and she couldn't blame him. Three of a kind was a strong hand. All Burke had was seven high, and the odds of him catching the four he needed for a straight were slim.

Except in Devil's Fork. Aggie knew the next card in her hand was the four he needed.

And beneath it, a junk card for Gabriel.

"Go ahead and deal, girlie," Burke said, grinning at her.

In that moment, she realized what was beneath the junk card. She could see it as clearly as if she'd been there all the times a soul had been lost before.

The four of spades went down in front of Burke. "Hot damn, a straight!" he yelled, drawing a cheer. Burke clapped Gabriel on the back, almost knocking him into the table. "Best hope that last two is waiting for you!"

Burke laughed, his grin mocking Aggie. Gabriel looked nervous, not worldly enough to recognize the trap he'd fallen into.

"Well, girl, let's see that last card," Burke demanded.

Aggie flipped the two of diamonds and laid it in front of Gabriel.

Fort McKinney, Wyoming, two years earlier

"When you're playing cards, if you've got a lot on the line, you want to be the dealer," Roche told Aggie, sitting across the table from her in the hospital. "You won't always get to be, but it's one of the best ways to keep folks from cheating you."

"How will they cheat?" Aggie asked, looking at the deck in his hands.

Roche grinned, then shuffled the deck before dealing five cards to each of them. Aggie picked hers up and looked at them. "Three kings. So?"

Without looking at his cards, Roche flipped them over to reveal four aces.

"That's called card mechanics," he told her. "You can close your mouth, by the way. Wouldn't want a bug to fly in there."

"How'd you do it?" Aggie asked.

"Quick hands and a shaved deck. Dealt some seconds too."

"I don't know what any of that means," Aggie said.

"You'll learn," Roche promised her. "I'll teach you."

Chapter 10

For a moment, there was no sound. Then Gabriel let out a sigh of relief.

"Thank God!"

The demons were looking at each other, raising eyebrows as they considered the cards on the table: Burke's straight, and Gabriel's four of a kind.

Aggie found herself staring down Burke, watching as the confusion in the demon's eyes turned to anger. Reaching across the table, he took the deck of cards from her hands and flipped over the next card.

The king of hearts.

The "Suicide King," named because the image on the card seemed to show the king stabbing himself with a dagger.

Aggie saw the symbolism and choked back a laugh. Gambling with these monsters was as good as suicide, so that card being the one that set a victim on the path to having their soul consumed was irony at its finest.

The demons around the table were whispering now, too low for Aggie to make out, but she knew it was something between astonishment and confusion. She wondered if they realized what she'd done, but knew they couldn't say anything without revealing their attempt to cheat Gabriel out of his soul.

Burke stared down at the Suicide King, then hurled the rest of the deck onto the table as he got to his feet.

"Come on," he growled. "We'll go see your damn priest."

The ride out to the waterfall looked different in daylight.

Ahead of them, the mountains came together, white and red rocks hiding beneath green and brown scrub. As they got closer, Aggie saw the canyon mouth, the river flowing over the falls before turning away from them. It was no longer the raging torrent it had been the night Padre was captured, and the sunlight glinted off the shallow water. There were even a few cottonwood trees growing on the banks.

If she hadn't known where she was, Aggie would have found it serene. But with Burke riding ahead of them and the still wide-eyed Gabriel riding next to her, she felt like the beauty was mocking her.

"I can't *believe* I got that two on the last draw," Gabriel said. "I thought I was a goner."

Aggie turned her head to glare at the monk. "I can't believe you opened your damn mouth after we agreed I'd be the one to do the talking."

He bowed his head. "I know. I shouldn't have, but they got me so riled up, I couldn't help but open my damn mouth."

"It almost cost you!" Aggie snapped, stealing a glance at the demon riding ahead of them. He was far enough, she doubted he could hear, and even if he could, what would he care?

"I know. It's funny though. No one was surprised when you turned the four to complete Burke's straight. But they were shocked when my two came up! I mean, it's a miracle that card was where it was, but they looked like they expected something else."

Aggie snorted. "A miracle ain't got nothing to do with it. They were expecting something else. The deck was stacked."

He looked at her, confusion in his blue eyes. "You stacked the deck?"

She shook her head. "*They* stacked the deck. Demon magic and all. I just turned it on its head and dealt the second card in for your last card."

Gabriel's jaw dropped. "It was a rigged game?"

"What the hell did you expect, playing cards with demons?"

The sound of the water tumbling over the rocks was getting louder as the trail came alongside the river.

He paused. "I should have known. I should have listened to you."

Damn it all! She didn't want to be too harsh, if she'd been in his shoes, she might have made the same mistake. Her papa had protected her, made sure she knew what she needed to survive out here. All Gabriel had was her, and apparently she hadn't made sure he was ready to face a town full of demons. "Ah, hell. At least you learned from it."

Gabriel nodded. "Don't gamble unless Aggie is the dealer."

Her eyes narrowed. "That wasn't the lesson." Then she saw the narrow grin on his face, and shook her head.

"I didn't know you had a sense of humor."

He shrugged. "I've spent my entire life around Padre; how could I not have a sense of humor?"

Aggie smiled at that.

"So how'd you learn how to deal cards like that?" Gabriel asked.

"My papa. He, well, it's a long story, but I didn't meet him until I was eighteen. After I found him, he spent six months in the hospital recovering from his injuries."

"You were that upset with him?" Gabriel asked.

Aggie looked angry for a moment, then chuckled when she saw Gabriel smile. "Not me. Some outlaws did a number on him and left him for dead. He'd been in the Army for years, so I took him to a nearby fort, and the doctor there saved him. But spending six months in a remote fort, we passed a lot of time playing cards and talking."

"That makes a little more sense," Gabriel said. "What happened to him?"

"He was tortured to death," Aggie said simply.

"Ah." Gabriel nodded. "And you want to save Padre because losing him feels like you're losing your father all over again."

Aggie felt angry for a moment, even though she knew he was right. Padre had been good to her, a friend, and she didn't know if she could stand to lose someone else.

"Yeah," she finally said.

They rode in silence for a little while.

"I'm sorry about your father," Gabriel said.

"Thank you." Aggie sighed. "Now let's see if we can figure out how to save Padre."

As they approached the waterfall, Burke steered his horse into the river. Aggie and Gabriel followed, their mounts plodding along the center of the stream. Approaching the thundering falls, Burke hissed something, and the waters parted like a curtain, revealing a path into the cave.

"Who goes there?" someone called from inside.

"It's Burke!"

Another demon appeared at the entry, red skinned and lanky. "I didn't expect anyone until the ceremony tonight."

"Yeah, well, the condemned has some visitors." Burke jerked his thumb over his shoulder at Aggie and Gabriel.

"We want to talk to him alone," Aggie said.

Burke laughed. "After the shit you've pulled?"

"Come on," Aggie said. "You can stand out here and watch, but you don't have to be close enough that we can smell you!"

Burke chuckled. "You don't like the smell of sulfur?"

"Fuck no," Aggie said.

"Best get used to it. The way you act, you're gonna be smelling it for all eternity."

"So I'll take the chance to avoid it now," Aggie shot back.

Burke sighed, then shook his head. "Get on out here, you and Murph. Let's give 'em some privacy."

He gestured toward the opening, and Aggie and Gabriel rode into the cave.

CHAPTER 11

Padre was standing in front of the altar, praying. When he heard their footsteps approaching, he turned around.

"Gabriel! Aggie! What are you doing here?" he asked.

"Padre!" Gabriel ran across the stone floor, footsteps echoing in the cavern. Aggie watched as Gabriel embraced Padre, tears flowing down the younger man's face.

"We'll find a way to save you," he said through the tears. "There's got to be something in one of the treaties; they can't do this!"

Padre stepped back, smiling at Gabriel. "Be calm, my son."

"Calm? There's no time for calm, they're going to kill you tonight!"

"And I'm ready to die."

Gabriel shook his head. "No. No, we have to do something."

"I have done something." Padre gently pushed past Gabriel and approached Aggie. "Hello, dear child. I'd hoped you'd gotten far away from this place."

She shrugged. "I was on my way, but I ran into Gabriel and realized he couldn't handle his rescue mission by himself."

A sorrowful smile. "I see. But I don't need to be rescued. My deal with the demons was simple: my soul for your freedom."

Behind Padre, Gabriel gasped as Aggie looked to the ground. "I didn't know."

"Of course not. They hoped you would do something to allow them to claim your soul in spite of our agreement." A twinkle appeared in his eye. "They're good at things like that."

"Padre," Gabriel said, looking at the altar.

"Yes, son?"

"You're giving them your soul?"

The priest shrugged. "It's what I had to offer."

Gabriel was studying the carvings on the rock altar. He looked up at them, his eyes wide. "She's not worth that."

"What?" Aggie stepped toward Gabriel with her hand raised. She was going to smack him into the altar and give him a good look at the carvings he was interested in.

"It's not an insult. I mean *no one's* worth that." Gabriel ignored the approaching threat, kneeling next to the altar. "These carvings are ancient Greek. 'The portal can only be opened by the sacrifice of a holy heart.' When they bind your soul to your heart, they'll be able to open the portal."

"Yeah, they were chanting about that the night they captured Padre," Aggie cut in. "Something about a holy one and the prince of darkness."

He nodded, not looking up at her. "I bet they've been using wicked hearts, sinners, their version of holy. But they've never had a priest before, and when they saw Padre, they figured out their mistake. Whatever deal he made, well, it wasn't worth it."

The priest sank to his knees. "Good God," he whispered. "What have I done?"

"So if this portal opens, what does it mean?" Aggie asked. "Demons everywhere?"

Gabriel shrugged. "I can't say for sure. Maybe they'll honor the treaties and stay in Devil's Fork."

"You know they won't," Padre said. "That many demons, those treaties won't be worth the paper they're written on. Everyone will be in danger."

"So what do we do?" Gabriel asked.

"We blow this shithole."

Padre and Gabriel turned to look at Aggie. "What?" Gabriel asked.

"We take your three sticks of dynamite and collapse the cave, portal and all."

"With dynamite?" Gabriel asked, walking back to his horse. Rummaging in the saddlebags, he found what he was looking for and brought back three sticks wrapped in wax paper. "I don't think this will stand up to hellfire," he said, looking down at the explosives.

Aggie remembered the sheriff, the way the cross had sunk into his flesh as the demon had screamed. She had an idea. "Bless it," she told Padre.

The priest's mouth dropped open. Then he grinned. "That's insane, but brilliant. I think it will work." He took the dynamite from Gabriel. Holding it in his left hand, he made the sign of the cross over it with his right as he whispered something in Latin. When he finished, he handed the dynamite to Aggie.

"Why are you giving it to her?" Gabriel asked.

"Because she's the only one small enough to squeeze through those chimneys."

"As long as you're blessing things..." Aggie took the gun from her belt and opened it, dropping the cartridge into her hand. Reaching into a leather pouch on her belt, she extracted her spare rounds.

A smile. Another sign of the cross and more Latin. Brother Gabriel reached into the pocket of his robe and took out a small vial of oil. Opening it, Padre splashed it on the metal cartridges.

"I wouldn't want to be on the receiving end of one of those," he said when he finished.

"I doubt the demons will either," Aggie said with a smile.

Padre turned to Gabriel. "Listen to Aggie, Gabriel. She has the—uh—*wisdom* to see this through."

Gabriel nodded, then stepped forward to embrace the priest. "I don't think I can do this."

Padre looked at Aggie and winked. "Give us a moment, please."

Green River, Wyoming, nine months earlier

Aggie and Roche were sitting in a hotel room, waiting for the sound of the train whistle. They'd received word the man they were after was coming to town, and they were staying out of sight until the train arrived so friends of his wouldn't see them and telegraph a warning up the line.

"I hate the waiting," Aggie said.

Roche looked up from his book. "You just need a hobby."

She shrugged. "I ain't a reader like you. Carryin' all them books around, your poor horse probably hates you."

He laughed. "We've got an understanding. But you don't have to read. There's other kinds of hobbies."

Aggie folded her arms over her chest. "Do I look like the knitting type?"

He shrugged, then went back to his book. Aggie watched him for a moment, then groaned.

"Damn waiting," she muttered.

"It could be worse," Roche said without looking up.

"How could it be worse?" Aggie asked.

"In the Army, they don't let you read while you wait..."

CHAPTER 12

The sun was setting when Aggie and Gabriel rode out of the cavern. Above them, streaks of color filled the sky, oranges, reds, and purples. It was beautiful, almost too beautiful for what was about to happen.

On the road, they could see the demons of Devil's Fork approaching.

"Might want to get on out of here," Burke said. "We'd let you stay in town, but no one's gonna be there to keep an eye on you."

"I think we'll make camp up the canyon a ways," Aggie said. "We wouldn't want to be a nuisance."

Burke stared at her for a moment, then laughed. "You seem to be a damn nuisance no matter where you are." He leaned in close to her. "Enjoy your last night. Come the morning, I'm going to kill you personally."

Aggie took the St. Christopher medallion and pressed it into his cheek. Burke jumped back, falling off his horse and into the river. Surfacing, he glared up at her, steam rising off the new scar on his cheek. "What the hell did you do that for?"

Aggie shrugged. "Just want to make sure I recognize you in the morning. Wouldn't want to let the wrong demon get me, ya know? Embarrassing for everyone, I'd think."

"Bitch," Burke muttered, getting to his feet.

Aggie turned her horse and rode away snickering, Gabriel splashing through the water behind her.

"Why are we coming up here?" Gabriel asked when Aggie had ridden around a bend in the canyon and swung off the sheriff's horse.

"We've got to get into the cavern to blow it up."

"How are you going to do that?" Gabriel asked.

She pointed to the overhang next to her, and the hole underneath it. "That's a chimney that leads down to the cavern. I'm going to make like Santa Claus and take a present down it."

As darkness fell, Aggie turned to Gabriel.

"You know how to shoot?" she asked.

He shook his head. "Monks aren't exactly known for their gunplay skills."

Aggie paused. "Was that a joke?"

He shrugged. "I thought it was the truth. I don't even think there was a gun in the monastery."

She shook her head. "Can you pull a trigger?"

He nodded.

"Then here." She pushed her gun belt into his hands. "If someone turns up to cause trouble, wait until they get close and you can't miss. Aim for the chest. Those blessed bullets will do the rest."

Even though she knew Gabriel needed to be armed to watch her back, that left Aggie with only the derringer behind her belt for protection. It wasn't a bad gun; it had saved her ass on multiple occasions, but with a short barrel and only two shots, it wasn't a lot of firepower for entering the demons' den.

It would have to do.

As she knelt under the outcropping, she heard chanting coming up from the cavern.

The ceremony was starting.

Using a rock to anchor a length of rope, she let the end fall into the hole, hoping it would reach the bottom. Stuffing the dynamite down the front of her shirt, she looked down the chimney at the flicker of light at the bottom. She didn't like having the dynamite that close to her, but it was better than dropping it down the chimney and hoping for the best.

Checking the rope, she nodded at Gabriel, then entered the chimney feet first.

The chimney was dark and cramped, with an almost vertical drop. Aggie was thankful for the rope; it was helping to control her descent. Rocks poked out, forcing her to contort her body to squeeze through. In the darkness, she was navigating by touch, not knowing what to expect from the next foot beneath her. Once, she got stuck, but managed to use the rope to pull herself out and tried a different position to slip past the outcropping.

Climbing out was going to be a bitch, she thought.

At least then she'd have an adrenaline rush to help her.

Finally, she reached the bottom of the shaft, the tunnel sloping down toward the cavern. Aggie crept down the slope, careful not to kick any loose rocks that might roll down the tunnel and announce her presence. The light from the cavern slowly illuminated the tunnel until finally, she reached the opening onto the ledge.

Aggie froze.

She wasn't alone.

A demon stood on the ledge, its back to her, watching the ceremony below.

CHAPTER 13

Staying as far back in the tunnel as she could, she pulled the dynamite from her shirt. The three sticks had been bound together, the fuses braided to make it easy to light all three quickly.

Setting the bundle on the tunnel floor, she drew the derringer and cocked it.

A lot of things would happen in a hurry.

In the chamber, she heard the grinding sound of the portal opening, and knew it was almost time.

Above her, up the chimney, she heard gunshots.

Gabriel!

She couldn't worry about him. Not now.

Aggie had her mission, Gabriel had his.

Slipping back to the mouth of the tunnel, she saw the demon on the ledge was still watching the events beneath them. The portal was halfway open, the chanting increasing in volume and speed.

She wanted to wait until the portal was fully open to throw the dynamite.

More gunfire came from up the passageway. Aggie ignored it. Whatever was going on up there didn't matter. Her work was down here.

She thought about Padre, sure his mangled body was just out of sight beneath the ledge, torn apart by the hell hounds.

Thinking about it hurt. He didn't deserve to have his body ripped apart and consumed, even if he was already dead and would never know.

It didn't stop her from being glad the dogs would be dead in a few moments, along with the demons.

Three-quarters of the way open. With her left hand, Aggie pulled a match from her pocket, then picked up the dynamite. The derringer felt tiny in her right hand, and from ten yards, it would probably be pushing her luck to get a kill shot.

But with the blessed bullet, she wasn't sure she had to kill the demon. Just hitting it would probably be enough to knock it off the ledge.

She hoped.

Another peek. The portal was still lowering, and Aggie found herself staring from the cavern into a flaming wasteland of fire and brimstone. Tortured souls, in the form of ghostly apparitions, lay helpless around a burning lake, screaming in agony as demons stood over them, laughing.

She shook her head. She couldn't help the souls of the damned.

It was her job to keep this world from becoming like the one she saw through the portal.

Aggie stepped out of the tunnel, raising the gun and aiming for the demon's head. It turned, quickly raising its hands when it saw her standing there.

It didn't matter.

Aggie pulled the trigger.

The sound of the gunshot was lost in the noise coming from hell. She saw the bullet clip the demon's shoulder. It put its hand to the wound, grimacing in pain, but it was still on its feet.

Still dangerous.

Cocking the gun again, Aggie aimed carefully, then fired the second barrel.

The bullet hit the demon in the gut. It stepped back, trying to absorb the impact, but there was nothing behind it. For a moment, the demon seemed to be trying to float, like the one Aggie saw the first time she was in the cave.

Then it disappeared over the edge.

Aggie stuck the derringer in her pocket, then struck the match and held it to the fuses, not daring to think about anything but her task. They caught, burning toward the explosives. She moved the dynamite to her right hand, then checked the portal's progress. As the opening reached the cavern floor, Aggie stepped to the brink of the ledge and hurled the dynamite toward the altar.

Then she ran.

Diving into the chimney, she scrambled up the incline. But there was no rope. The chimney kept sloping up.

A horrific realization hit her as an explosion echoed in the cave behind her.

She'd climbed into the wrong chimney.

Aggie had no choice. She scrambled up the passage, this one much wider, a gently sloping tunnel held up with splintering timbers that smelled of rot. Probably an old mine shaft.

Around her, the rock shook, and a collapse seemed imminent, so she focused on putting as much distance between her and the cavern as she could.

Crashing sounds behind her suggested the explosion had collapsed not only the portal, but the whole chamber, altar and all.

Aggie pushed herself to move even faster, feeling her way through the darkness. A pile of rocks on the floor tripped her, but she got back on her feet and kept scrambling, fearing that if she stopped, the cracks in the rocks might catch up to her and bring the shaft down on her.

Finally, she saw stars ahead of her, caught a whiff of fresh night air, and a moment later, she sprinted into the moonlight.

Skidding to a stop, she put her hands on her knees, panting as she tried to catch her breath. Behind her, the rumblings slowed to a stop.

As she stood, she looked around and realized she was farther up the canyon, across the river from the trail. But she'd done it. She'd brought down the portal, stopped hell from coming to earth.

Now she only had one question to answer:

What happened to Gabriel?

Chapter 14

Splashing across the river, Aggie ran downhill to where she'd left Gabriel.

Rounding a bend in the canyon, she gasped. The waterfall had collapsed, leaving a stretch of rapids in its place. Water roared over the rocks, tumbling downriver past where the entrance had been.

Gabriel was lying on the riverbank, not moving. Standing over him was... "You!" Aggie yelled, reaching for her gun, then realizing it was gone.

She'd given it to Gabriel before descending into the cavern. Did he still have it? Or had he lost it in the process of whatever had happened to him.

Burke turned, a wicked grin gleaming in the moonlight. "Me." The demon raised his gun, pointing it at Gabriel. "He ain't dead, but if you don't play nice, he will be."

Aggie slowly raised her hands. "Why weren't you in the cave?"

"Knowing you were out here?" He shook his head. "I knew you were trouble when you killed the sheriff, and I knew you were smarter than you looked when you foiled my plan at the poker game. I knew you'd be up to something tonight. I just hoped it'd play to my advantage."

"Your advantage?" Aggie asked. Gabriel was starting to stir behind the demon, and Aggie wanted to keep the demon's attention on her. If he realized Gabriel was coming to, he might hurt him even worse than whatever he'd done the first time. "I'd figure opening a portal to hell would be to your advantage."

Burke laughed. "Fuck no. You think I want a bunch of demons running around, making souls even harder to come by, having Satan looking over my damn shoulder?" He shook his head. "This goddamn place is even better now that you've gotten rid of every stupid fucker who wanted that. I'm obliged to you, actually. Part of the reason I haven't consumed his soul." He jerked a thumb toward Gabriel.

"I was wondering about that," Aggie said as Gabriel lifted his head. "Why are we still alive?"

The demon turned his gun toward Aggie. "Actually, I ain't got much use for you anymore, now that you mention it. The monk'll be an asset, though. He knows how the church works, and I can use that information to make a new deal with the bishop."

Gabriel was on his knees. He reached down and picked something up.

Her gun.

He did still have it.

Aggie fought to keep from grinning. "You think I'm going to let you consume my soul?" she asked. "I'd just as soon blow my own brains out."

Burke laughed. "A mortal sin, as the priests say. Not that you'd escape me. I know a few tricks, see."

"Resurrection?" Aggie asked as Gabriel raised the gun, aiming it at the demon.

"Do I look like the son of God?" He held both hands out to show her his red palms, letting his gun go slack and laughing again.

Gabriel fired.

The grin never left Burke's face. He stood for a moment, silhouetted in the moonlight, then fell forward, landing face down in the rocky soil.

Aggie drew her derringer before approaching the body. Black blood oozed out of a hole in the back of the demon's head, the red skin around the wound showing signs of charring.

The last demon was dead.

Aggie ran to Gabriel. "Are you okay?"

"My head," he whispered. "He snuck up behind me, hit me over the head. I'm sorry."

"Don't be," Aggie smiled. "You just saved my life."

Gabriel nodded, then looked around at the changed landscape. "So did it work?"

"Yep. I blew the portal to hell," Aggie said. "Along with the rest of the demons. Just like we planned."

He looked around, the shock on his face slowly changing to a grin.

"I'd say Devil's Fork just became a ghost town."

The next morning, Aggie woke to the smell of coffee brewing. Rubbing the sleep from her eyes, she climbed out of her bedroll and got to her feet.

Gabriel had built a fire, a coffee pot sitting among the coals, but he was not with it. She found him by the river, casting a line into the water.

"Good morning," she said.

Gabriel turned, a smile lighting up his face. "Good morning! I'm just trying to catch us some breakfast." He pointed to a creel with two fish already on it. "I'm not Jesus, so I have to multiply the fish the hard way."

Aggie chuckled, seeing the monk in a new light. While his ineptitude had been a challenge, they'd managed to overcome it, and now that Padre was gone, she felt a kinship to him.

Almost like Gabriel was her problem now.

"Oh, I caught something else," he said, jerking his head.

Tied to a cottonwood tree on the riverbank was Gato alongside Padre's horse.

"Where did you come from?" Aggie asked, walking over to stroke her horse's neck.

"They came wandering down the trail this morning, almost like they knew the demons were gone," Gabriel said, coming over to join her. "I recognized Padre's horse, and figured the other was probably yours."

"Gato. His name is Gato," Aggie said with a smile.

"A horse named cat." Gabriel shook his head, but smiled back at her.

"That's what Padre said." Aggie smiled. "I guess they knew they should stick together."

Gabriel looked at her, then down at his feet, then took a deep breath. Aggie could tell he wanted to ask something, but didn't have the nerve.

"So what happens next?" Aggie asked as they walked back to the fire, trying to lead the question from him. "Are you going back to the monastery?"

Gabriel shook his head. "I don't think I can, after what happened. Losing Padre is hard, and in the process, I abandoned my vows and committed enough sins to make one of those demons look like a saint! Not to mention that with everything I know about Devil's Fork now, what the church *let* those demons do to people, I'm going to have a hard time looking the bishop in the eye."

Aggie sat down on a rock. "So what will you do?"

He sighed. "Padre and I talked about that. There's not a lot of use for what you learn as a monk in the world. Mostly, I want to explore, to find out what life is like outside the monastery walls."

A nod. "I can understand that."

"But I'm not ready for the real world. I don't have the experience to survive. Last night, before that demon whacked me, I kept shooting at shadows. Being alone and vulnerable, it felt like the whole world was a threat."

Aggie smiled. "That's actually pretty close to right. It ain't easy being alone out here."

"You're alone," Gabriel pointed out.

"Not by choice," Aggie said, thinking again of her papa. That memory would always linger, springing up when she wasn't ready for it. "You shouldn't be alone either, not after losing someone you care about. That only makes it harder."

Gabriel turned to look at her. He opened his mouth, closed it, then started to say something, then stopped.

"Are you going to say something, or keep exercising your jaw?" Aggie asked.

He sighed. "Padre suggested I ask if I can ride with you."

There it was. The question she'd hoped was coming, even though she hadn't wanted to admit it to herself.

"On one condition."

"What's that?" He looked nervous.

"We stop in Devil's Fork and find you some new clothes." Aggie nodded at his robe. "You can't ride in those robes for shit."

Laramie, Wyoming, eight months earlier

Aggie and Roche sat on their horses in a small cave, watching as the rain beat down outside.

"This ain't the best weather I've seen," Aggie said.

Roche laughed. "But the company's pretty good. If you find someone you can tolerate, the weather don't matter much."

Aggie smiled at him. "I think you're pretty damn easy to tolerate."

Roche grinned. "Why, thank you—"

"I know that damn look," Aggie cut him off. "Don't even think about saying something smart!"

"Too late, done thought about it."

Aggie rolled her eyes. "Sometimes you're easier to tolerate than others."

Roche laughed. "But it'd be awful boring without me."

Acknowledgements

Alright. Time for me to try to remember everyone (and inevitably forget a bunch of people) I need to acknowledge.

Thank you to my loving wife, Anna, for not taking inspiration from my work for a creative way to deal with myself or the children.

Thank you to Atlas and Wednesday for jumping on the bed when I'm trying to write and adding their own "edits" to my work (if you see a typo, Wednesday was there).

Thank you to Rebecca and Cyan, my partners at Undertaker Books, without whom you definitely wouldn't be seeing this.

Thank you to Desiree Horton for beta reading and suggesting an important change that made the novella better.

Thank you to C.M. Saunders, Brennan LaFaro, Desiree Horton, and Ann O'Mara Heyward for providing blurbs.

Thank you to Milt Theodossiou for the early review and feedback.

Thank you to Beth, Joe, Amy, and Marteena at Writer's Group for the love and support.

Thank you to my readers, for taking a chance on Indie Western Horror!

And thank you to anyone I've forgotten!

About D.L. Winchester

D.L. Winchester lives in the foothills of southern Appalachia. A former mortician, his work searches the darkness to find tales worth telling. He is the author of over three hundred obituaries, numerous short stories, the novella *The Screaming House,* and the collections *Shadows of Appalachia* and *A Terrible Place and Other Flashes of Horror.* In his spare time, he can be found searching for inspiration in the world around him and trying to keep his children from becoming the next generation of horror villains.

ALSO BY D.L. WINCHESTER

A Terrible Place and Other Flashes of Darkness

Cabin Nine

Marigolds

Shadows of Appalachia: A Short Story Chapbook

The Screaming House

The Unknown Leon

UB Website

If you are a fan of horror stories and tales,
you'll want to follow Undertaker Books.
We're bringing you stories to take to your grave.

www.ingramcontent.com/pod-product-compliance
Lightning Source LLC
Chambersburg PA
CBHW030942310726
48969CB00008B/2350